My name is
STARDUST

Written by Bailey & Douglas Harris

Illustrated by Natalie Malan

Hello, everyone!
My name is Stardust.
It's nice to meet you.

Do you know what Earth is made of?
Do you know what YOU are made of?
Well, if not, then today is your lucky day!

Throughout the history of our universe, countless billions of stars have formed and then exploded, leaving tiny specks of dust all over space.

About 4.6 billion years ago, dust from some of those exploded stars came together to make up our solar system.

Our solar system is made of stardust!

There are more than a hundred billion galaxies in our universe. And there are hundreds of billions of stars in each galaxy!

There are more stars in our universe than there are grains of sand on Earth. Our Sun is one of those billions and billions of stars.

There are eight planets in our solar system. The four inner planets are Mercury, Venus, Earth, and Mars.

Mars

Earth

Venus

Mercury

Neptune

Uranus

Saturn

Jupiter

The outer planets are called gas giants. They are Jupiter, Saturn, Uranus, and Neptune.

The planets are made of stardust!

Earth looks like a little blue ball when you look at it from far away in space. It is so beautiful.

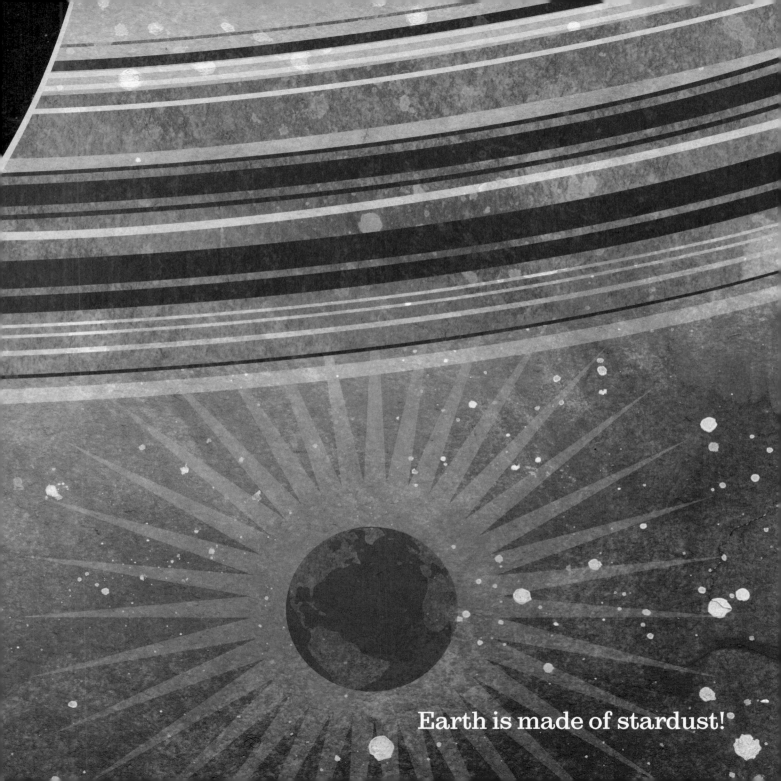

Earth is made of stardust!

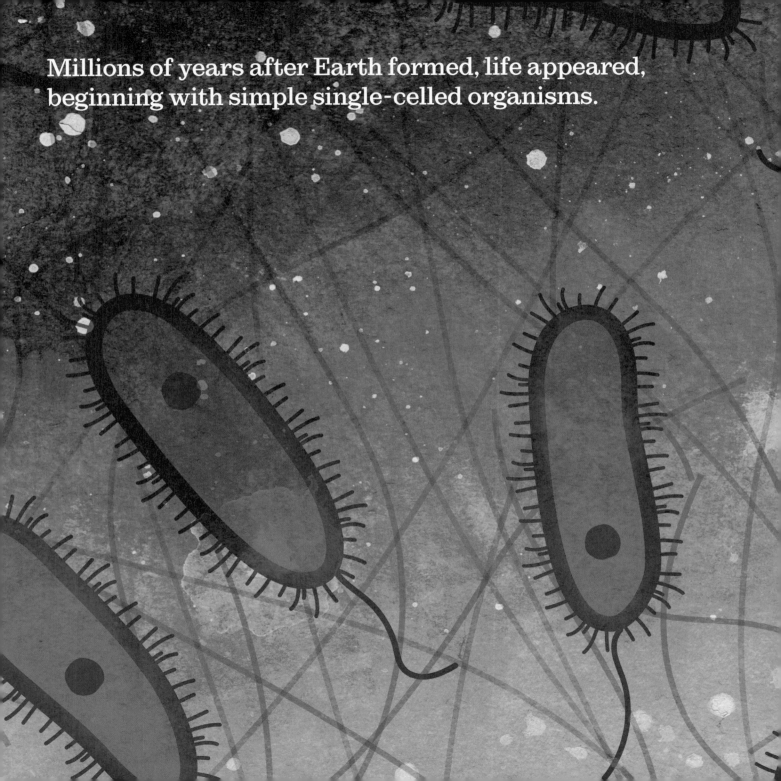

Millions of years after Earth formed, life appeared, beginning with simple single-celled organisms.

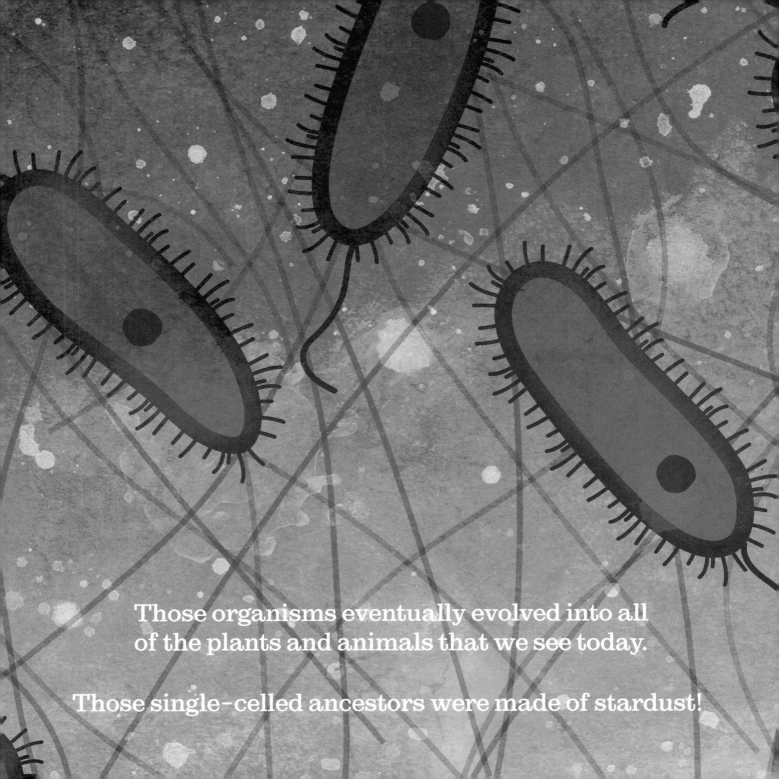

Those organisms eventually evolved into all of the plants and animals that we see today.

Those single-celled ancestors were made of stardust!

Tiktaalik is one of my favorite ancient creatures.
Tiktaalik lived about 375 million years ago.

Tiktaalik was a fish with scales and
gills, but it also had wrist bones, ribs,
lungs, and a neck.

Tiktaalik could raise its body up out of the shallow water where it lived. Fossils like Tiktaalik show us how fish evolved into animals that walk on land, like crocodiles.

Tiktaalik was made of stardust!

Dinosaurs lived on Earth millions of years ago. My favorite dinosaur is the Brachiosaurus. Brachiosaurus was so tall that it could eat the leaves from the top of very high trees. It looked a little strange because its front legs were longer than its back legs, but that is one of the reasons it's my favorite.

Brachiosaurus was 85 feet long and weighed 40 tons (that's heavier than five elephants)!

Brachiosaurus was made of LOTS of stardust!

Around 65 million years ago, soon after dinosaurs became extinct, there lived a small mammal called Purgatorius. Purgatorius was about the size of a rat or mouse.

Humans did not exist yet. Most mammals at that time were very small, like Purgatorius. Those early mammals evolved into all the later kinds of mammals, everything from bats to whales to primates like monkeys and apes.

Purgatorius was made of stardust!

Unicorns lived on earth a long
time ago with pixies and fairies.

Just kidding. There's no evidence
of real unicorns, pixies, or fairies.

But if they were real, they would be made of stardust!

Lucy was one of the first apelike animals that walked upright much like we humans do now.

She lived about 3.2 million years ago in Africa,
where her fossil bones were found in 1974.

Lucy was made of stardust!

I was born nine years ago and I am
growing bigger and bigger each year.

I love to sing, dance, and paint.
I am made of stardust!

And so are
YOU!

Glossary

Universe: everything that exists including the solar system, the galaxies, and the space between the galaxies.

Sun: the earth's star, located in the middle of our solar system.

Solar System: a star and all the objects that orbit it including planets and their moons.

Galaxy: a group of billions of stars held together by gravity, like the Milky Way.

Planet: a large round object that orbits a star.

Cell: a small unit of plant or animal life, having a nucleus and surrounded by a very thin membrane.

Organism: an individual living thing, such as a plant, animal, or bacterium.

Evolve: to develop or change over time.

Evidence: something that gives proof or a reason to believe.

Fossil: the preserved remains or traces of an ancient animal or plant.

Mammal: an animal that is warm-blooded, has fur or hair, has a skeleton inside its body, and feeds its young with milk produced by the mother.

Extinct: a plant or animal species that no longer exists in living form.

Primates: an order of mammals that includes humans, monkeys, and apes.

Please refer to SbgPublishing.com for references.

For Bryson, McKay, Bailey, and Elle
D.H.

For my mom, MacKenzie Harris
B.H.

To my constant source of inspiration: Penny, Emmett, Calvin and Alice.
N.M.

A special thank you to ~

Dr. Eric Meikle, former Education Project Director
at the National Center for Science Education, for his invaluable help in
editing for scientific accuracy and general content.

Dr. Michael Shermer and his son, Vincent, who was the inspiration for
our sweet pixie baby.

StoryBook Genius
Publishing
SbgPublishing.com

expanding minds
opening hearts
igniting curiosity

Book design that makes you go yippee!
yipjar.com

CPSIA information can be obtained at www.ICGtesting.com
Printed in the USA
LVIW01n1433190517
534691LV00001B/6